THIS WALKER BOOK BELONGS TO:

_____

_____

_____

_____

For
Smail Cifric
1961–1990

First published 1993 by Walker Books Ltd
87 Vauxhall Walk, London, SE11 5HJ

This edition published 1995

3 4 5 6 7 8 9 10

© 1993 David Hughes

This book has been typeset in Calligraphic.

Printed in Hong Kong

British Library Cataloguing in Publication Data
A catalogue record for this book is available
from the British Library
ISBN 0-7445-3624-3

BULLY

by

David Hughes

WALKER BOOKS

AND SUBSIDIARIES

LONDON • BOSTON • SYDNEY

It was a lovely day.

Everyone was playing.

Penguin was playing with Pig.

Elephant was playing with Girl and Teddy.

Boy was playing with Crocodile.

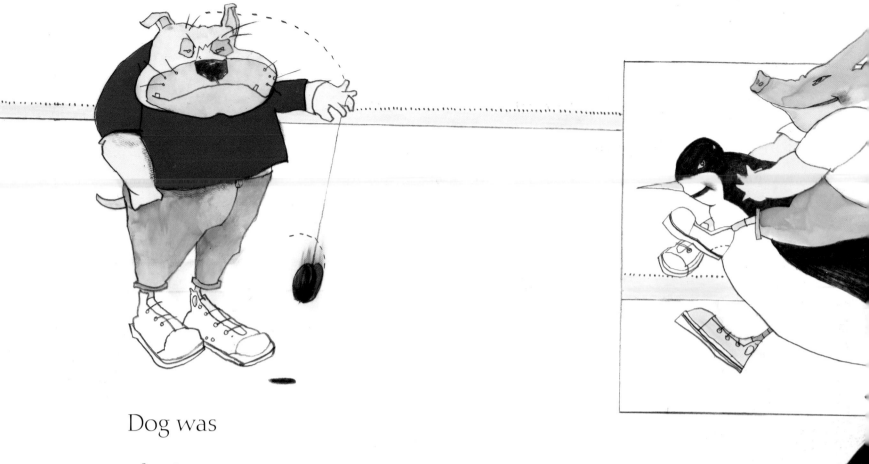

Dog was

playing

on his

own.

"Hey, Penguin," Dog called. "Let's kick Teddy."
Pig smiled a revolting smile.

"Why?" Girl asked.

"Because he's furry," Penguin said.

"BULLY," Girl said.

Pig kicked Teddy.

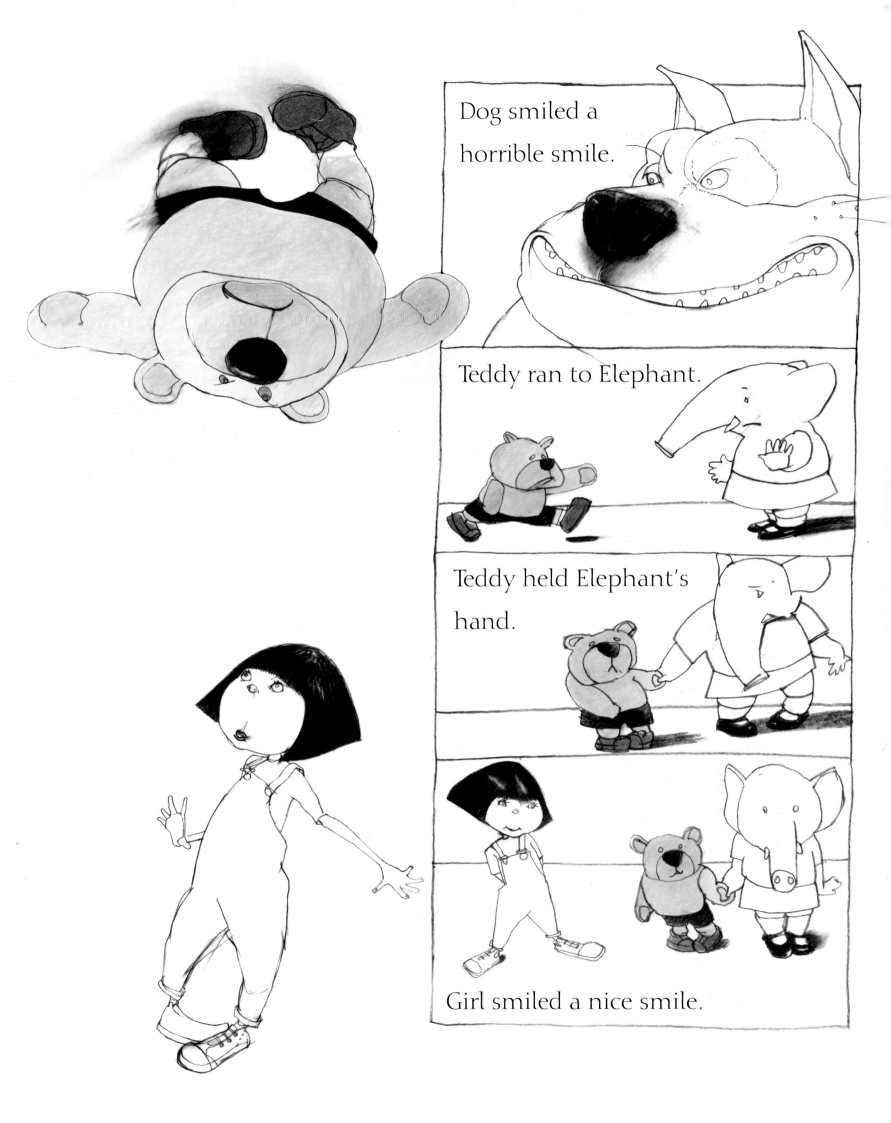

Dog smiled a horrible smile.

Teddy ran to Elephant.

Teddy held Elephant's hand.

Girl smiled a nice smile.

"Hey, Penguin,"   Dog called. "Let's kick Elephant."

"Because she's got big ears," Penguin said.

Elephant ran to Girl.   Elephant held

Boy grinned.   Pig smiled a revolting smile.   "Why?" Girl asked.

Boy kicked Elephant.   Dog smiled a horrible smile.

Girl's hand.   Teddy smiled a nice smile.

"Hey, Penguin," Dog called. "Let's kick Girl."

Penguin smiled a horrible smile. Boy grinned.

Pig smiled a revolting smile.

"Why?" Girl asked.

"Because you keep asking why," Penguin said.

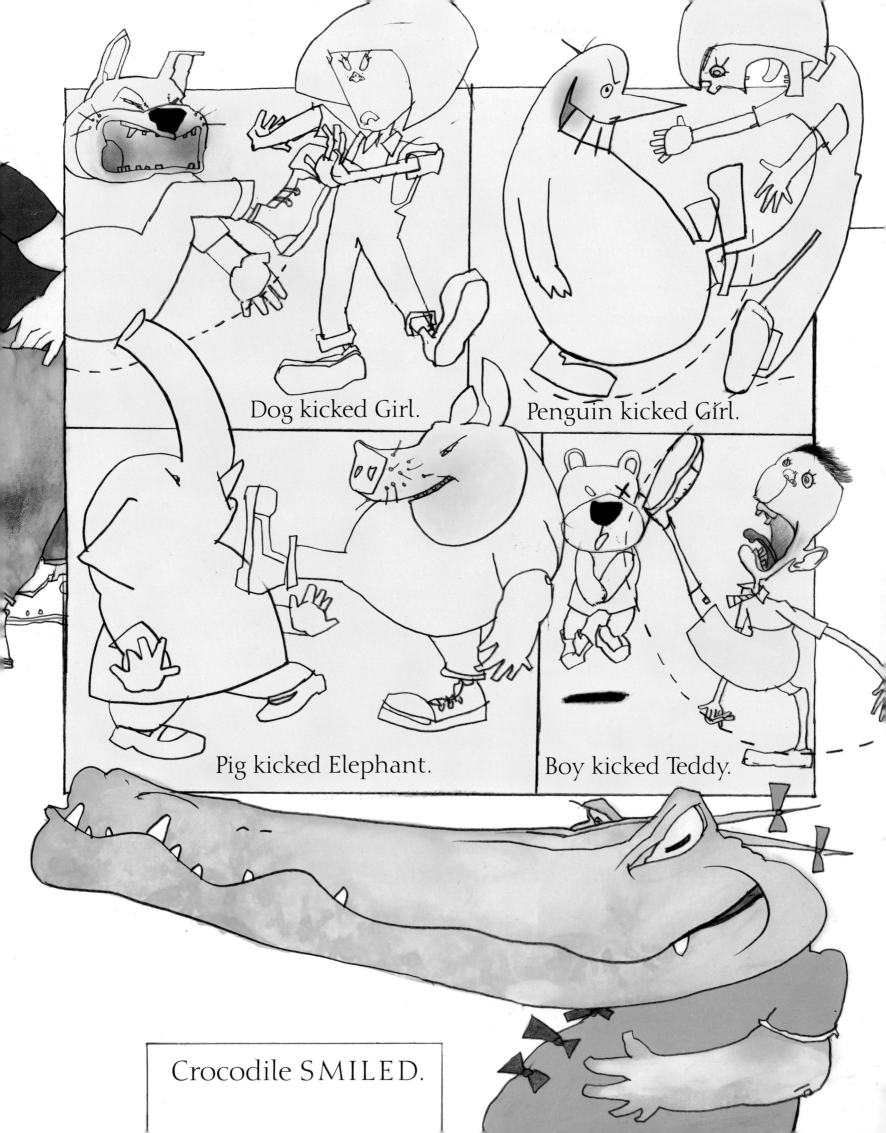

Dog kicked Girl.

Penguin kicked Girl.

Pig kicked Elephant.

Boy kicked Teddy.

Crocodile SMILED.

"Hey, Penguin,"
Dog called. "Let's kick Crocodile."
Crocodile still smiled.
"Because she's smiling," Penguin said.
Crocodile still smiled.

Pig kicked Crocodile.

Dog kicked Crocodile.

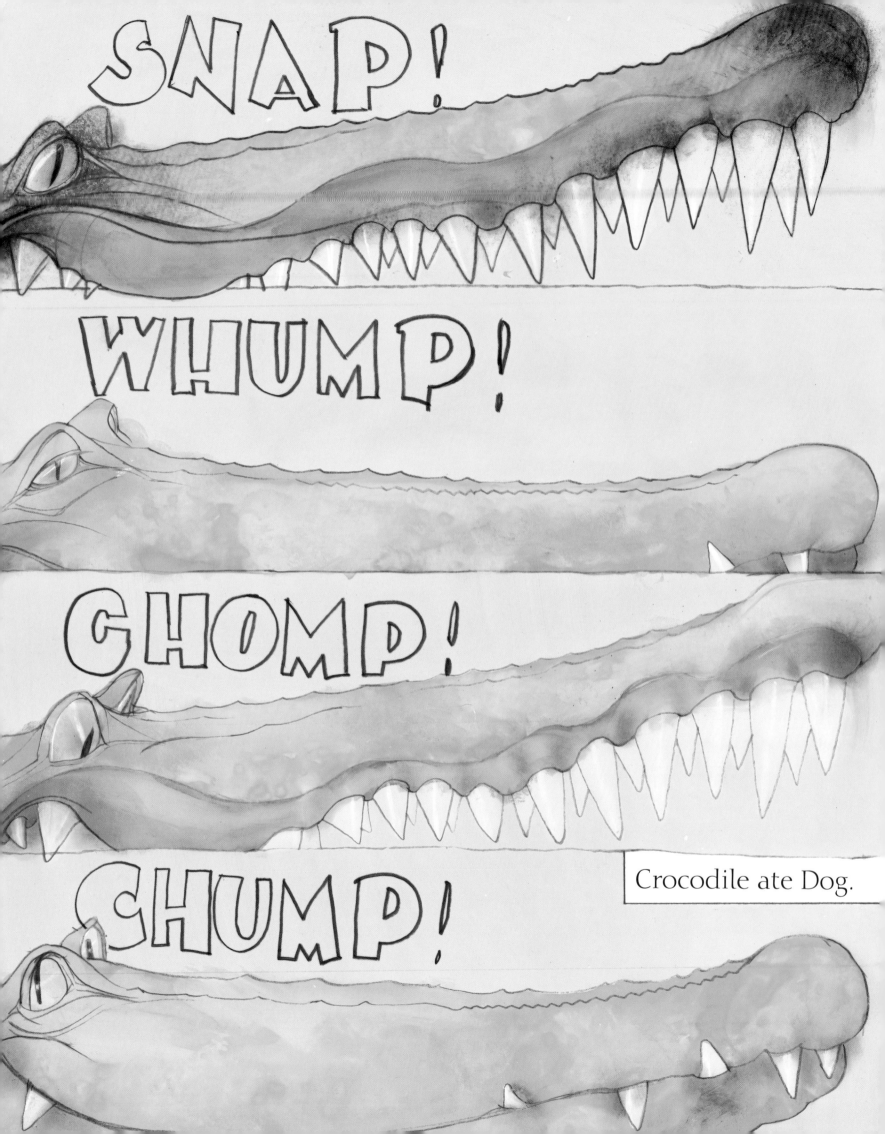

Crocodile ate Dog.

Crocodile ate Pig.

Everyone went wild.

SNAP! WHUMP! CHOMP! CHUMP!

Everyone played Bully.

SNAP! WHUMP!

SNAP!
...WHUMP!
CHOMP!
...CHUMP!

Crocodile ate Teddy.

...SNAP!
WHUMP!
CHOMP!
...CHUMP!

Crocodile ate Elephant.

Crocodile burped.
Penguin smiled a creepy smile.
"Stop it!" Girl shouted.
"Shut up!" Boy said,
and kicked Girl.
"BULLY!" Girl said.

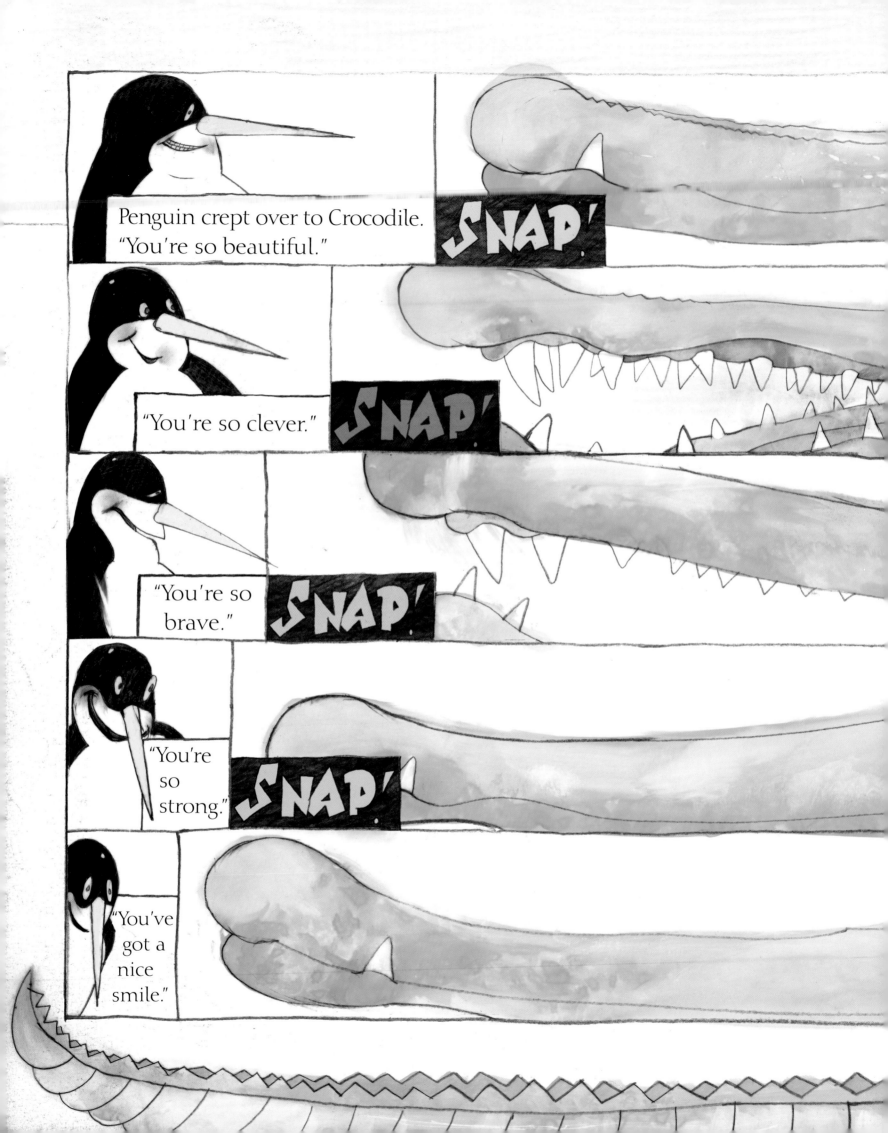

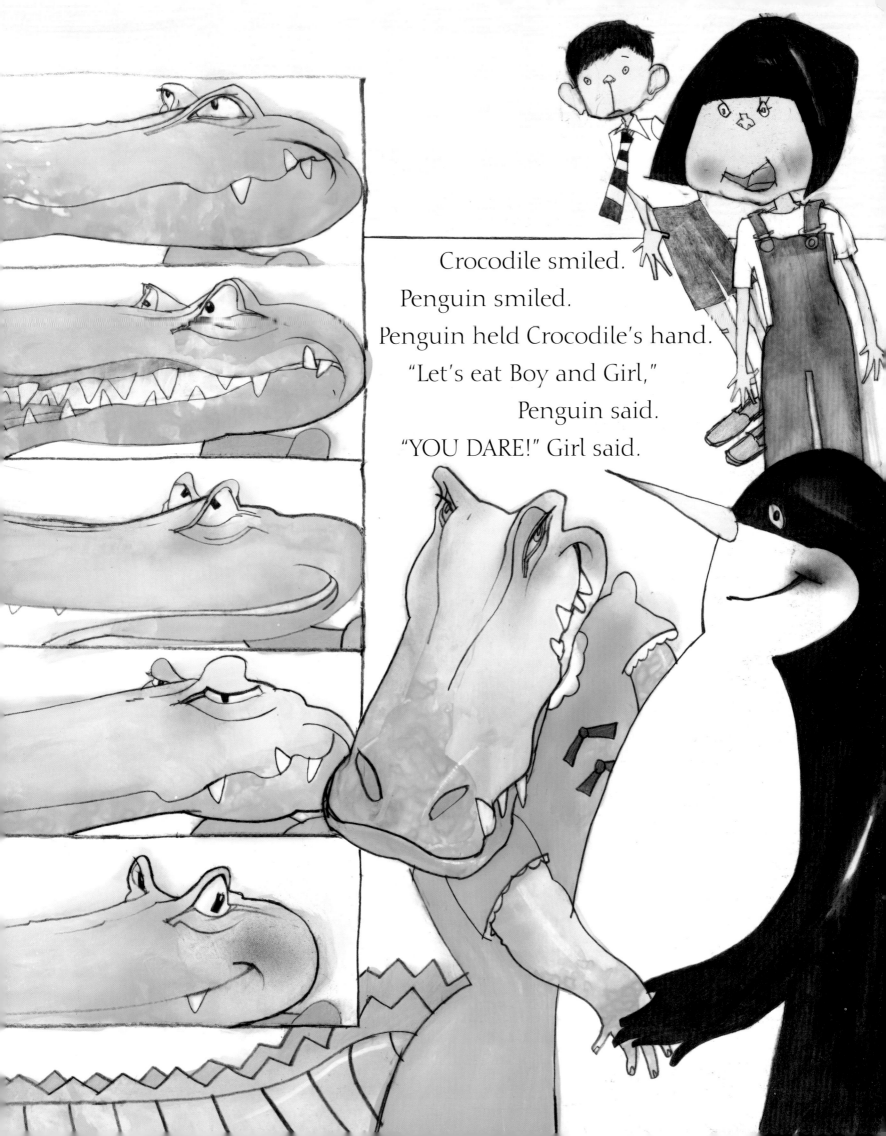

Crocodile smiled.
Penguin smiled.
Penguin held Crocodile's hand.
"Let's eat Boy and Girl,"
Penguin said.
"YOU DARE!" Girl said.

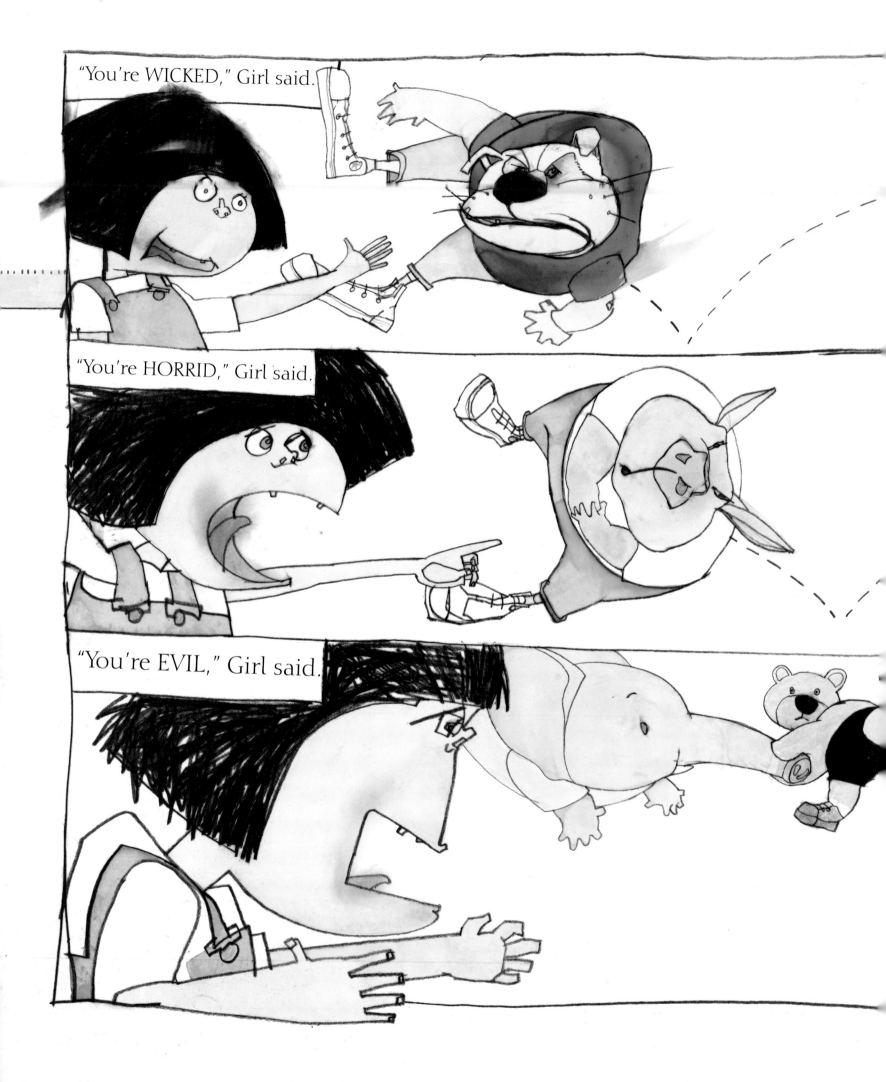

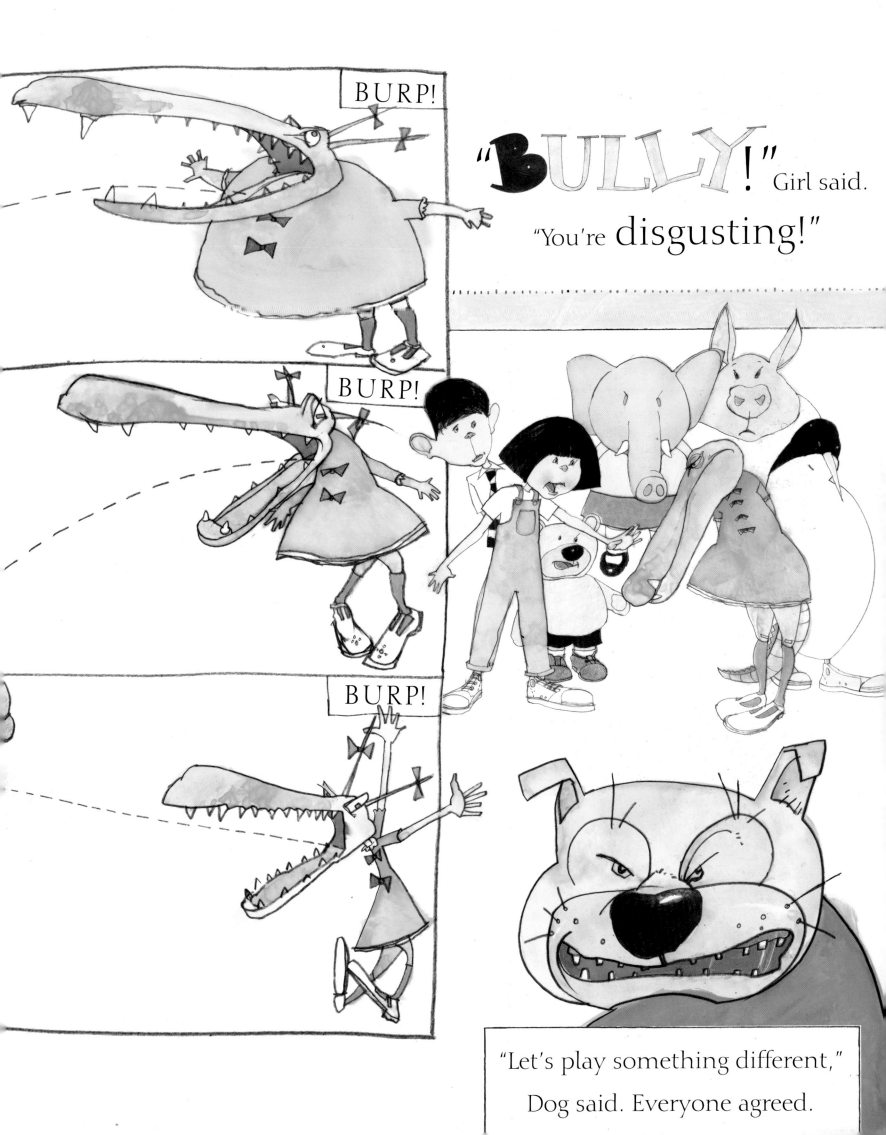

BURP!

"BULLY!" Girl said.

"You're **disgusting!**"

BURP!

BURP!

"Let's play something different,"
Dog said. Everyone agreed.

Look! Everyone is playing again.

Isn't it a lovely day?